THE TWISTER TRAP

BY MICHAEL DAHL
ILLUSTRATED BY BRADFORD KENDALL

Librarian Reviewer
Laurie K. Holland
Media Specialist (National Board Certified), Edina, MN
MA in Elementary Education, Minnesota State University, Mankato

Reading Consultant
Elizabeth Stedem
Educator/Consultant, Colorado Springs, CO
MA in Elementary Education, University of Denver, CO

STONE ARCH BOOKS
Minneapolis   San Diego

Zone Books are published by Stone Arch Books,
151 Good Counsel Drive, P.O. Box 669,
Mankato, Minnesota 56002.
www.stonearchbooks.com

Library of Congress Cataloging-in-Publication Data
Dahl, Michael.
    The Twister Trap / by Michael Dahl; illustrated by Bradford
Kendall.
    p. cm. — (Zone Books — Library of Doom)
    ISBN 978-1-4342-0488-2 (library binding)
    ISBN 978-1-4342-0548-3 (paperback)
    [1. Books and reading—Fiction. 2. Librarians—Fiction.
3. Fantasy.] I. Kendall, Bradford, ill. II. Title.
PZ7.D15134Twi 2008
[Fic]—dc22   2007032224

Summary: The Page Turners, two powerful books from the Library
of Doom, have fallen into the hands of an evil magician. He turns
the books into two terrible tornadoes, to destroy the Librarian.
But when the twisters suddenly head toward a small village, the
Librarian must risk his life to stop them.

Creative Director: Heather Kindseth
Senior Designer for Cover and Interior: Kay Fraser
Graphic Designer: Brann Garvey

1 2 3 4 5 6 12 11 10 09 08 07

Printed in the United States of America.

TABLE OF CONTENTS

The Library of Doom is the world's largest collection of strange and dangerous books. The Librarian's duty is to keep the books from falling into the hands of those who would use them for evil purposes.

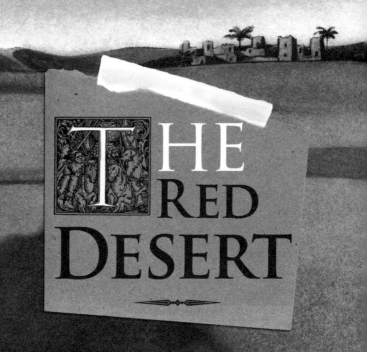

CHAPTER 1

THE RED DESERT

A strange <u>shadow</u> passes through a vast, red desert.

The shadow belongs to an **evil magician.** He is known as the Spellbinder.

Under his arms are two strange books, the magical Page Turners.

The books were stolen from the Library of Doom.

When he reaches the middle of the desert, the Spellbinder digs **two holes** in the soft sand.

He lays a book in each hole.
Then he **covers** them with `sand`.

The Spellbinder chuckles.

A gentle `breeze blows` across
the sand.

CHAPTER 2

THE
PAGE
TURNERS

The wind grows **stronger** and **stronger** and spins above the two buried books.

The breeze turns into **two** **powerful twisters.**

The Spellbinder **laughs.**

"These Page Turners will bring the Librarian here," he says. "And they will **destroy him!**"

The Librarian has been following the Spellbinder.

He must find the **stolen** books and return them to the Library of Doom.

They are <u>**too powerful**</u> to be loose in the world.

The Librarian sees two tall twisters in the distance.

He knows these storms are caused by the **Page Turners.**

The **Spellbinder** must be near.

CHAPTER 3

THE VILLAGE

A few children in a small desert village are playing.

The sky becomes **dark.**

One boy looks up and points.

"A sandstorm!" he shouts.

The **twisters spin** toward the village.

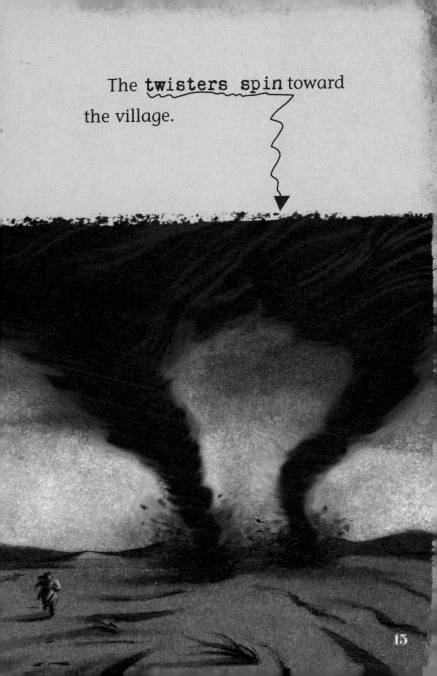

The wind **blows stronger**.
The sky is red, like **blood**.

Sand **whips** through the village.

It stings the villagers' hands
and faces.

As the twisters swirl closer, the
people **run for shelter**.

The **roof blows** off of a building.

It flies toward the **running** boy.

The boy crouches down to hide.

Somewhere, a mother **screams.**

Suddenly, a dark shape flies out of the blowing sand.

It is the Librarian.

He pulls the boy to safety. A
moment later, the roof `crashes`
behind them.

Then the Librarian **leaps** into
one of the swirling twisters.

He must find a way to stop
them.

CHAPTER 4

INTO THE STORM

Wind **screams** in his ears. Sand scratches his face and arms.

The Librarian cannot fight the powerful, **twisting air.**

22

The twister pulls the Librarian
into its **mighty grip.**

The Librarian cannot see.

He cannot hear anything except
the **screaming wind.**

The wind throws the Librarian
through the air as if he were a
broken puppet.

The Librarian **crashes**
against the wall of a house.

CHAPTER 5

A GRAVE OF SAND

The boy **runs** to the Librarian.

"Hurry," says the boy. "You can't stay here. The sand will **bury** you."

The Librarian is **battered** and **bruised**.

He can hardly **hear** the boy.

But he does hear one word.

Bury.

The Librarian crawls to his knees.

He has an **idea.**

He sees the **twisters** spin
closer to the village.

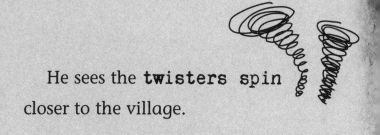

Then the Librarian begins
to **dig**.

He lays down in the **path** of the twisters.

He covers himself with the **red** sand.

The boy cannot see where the
Librarian went.

All he can see is the twisters as
they burst into the village.

Suddenly, two powerful arms rise out of the sand.

The Librarian holds the two Page Turners in his hands.

The books were moving beneath the sand, guiding the twisters above them.

In the hands of their guardian, the books are now calm.

The winds in the village die away.

The red sky clears.

The Spellbinder's evil plan has been defeated.

On a distant desert hill, an angry shadow turns away.

A PAGE FROM THE LIBRARY OF DOOM

MORE ABOUT DESERT STORMS

A sandstorm is caused by strong winds blowing across the surface of a desert or sandy region of earth.

Sandstorms in Africa's Sahara Desert can blow dust and sand as far away as the United States and Greenland.

Scientists have found desert sand on top of the Alps, Europe's highest mountains. They claim the sand had come from sandstorms.

A Sahara sandstorm is known as a **simoom** (suh-MOOM) or **simoon** (suh-MOON).

Sandstorms are deadly. The rough sand can blow against plants and destroy them. Sand particles can also get in the eyes, noses, and lungs of animals and humans.

A sandstorm known as the **leveche** (luh-VAY-chay) blows red Sahara dust across the sea and into Spain. The winds can reach 60 mph (100 kpm) and last four days!

Ancient legends say that a Persian army of 50,000 soldiers was caught in an Egyptian sandstorm in 521 BC. The entire army was buried in the sand and the bodies were never found.

ABOUT THE AUTHOR

Michael Dahl is the author of more than
100 books for children and young adults.
He has twice won the AEP Distinguished
Achievement Award for his nonfiction. His
Finnegan Zwake mystery series was chosen
by the Agatha Awards to be among the
five best mystery books for children in 2002
and 2003. He collects books on poison and
graveyards, and lives in a haunted house in
Minneapolis, Minnesota.

ABOUT THE ILLUSTRATOR

Bradford Kendall has enjoyed drawing for
as long as he can remember. As a boy,
he loved to read comic books and watch
old monster movies. He graduated from
the Rhode Island School of Design with a
BFA in Illustration. He has owned his own
commercial art business since 1983, and
lives in Providence, Rhode Island, with his
wife, Leigh, and their two children Lily
and Stephen. They also have a cat named
Hansel and a dog named Gretel.

GLOSSARY

battered (BAT-uhrd)—to be injured by being hit over and over again

chuckle (CHUH-kul)—to laugh quietly

crouches (KROUCH-ez)—gets close to the ground by bending at the knees

defeated (di-FEE-tuhd)—beaten or destroyed by someone else

guardian (GAR-dee-uhn)—someone who protects another person or object

sandstorm (SAND-storm)—strong winds in the desert that blow around lots of sand

twisters (TWISS-turz)—another name for tornadoes, a storm with a violent tunnel of wind that can destroy objects on the ground

vast (VAST)—an extremely large area

village (VIL-ij)—a group of houses or a community that is smaller than a town

DISCUSSION QUESTIONS

1. The Librarian saved the small village and stopped the evil Page Turners. If he could've only done one or the other, what decision would he have made? Explain your answer.

2. At the end of the story, the Spellbinder's plans are defeated. What happened after his plan failed? Do you think he will come after the Librarian again? Why or why not?

3. Illustrations can make a book more exciting. What is your favorite illustration in this book? What did you like about it? How did it make the book more exciting?

WRITING PROMPTS

1. Write a story about your own experience with a storm or bad weather. Was it rain, lightning, thunder, or worse? How did you and your family stay safe?

2. Use your imagination and write more about the Spellbinder character. What is his real name? Where did he grow up? How did he become so evil?

3. The author never reveals what the stories inside the Page Turner books are about. Pretend you are the author of the Page Turners and describe the stories in those books.

INTERNET SITES

The book may be over, but the adventure is just beginning.

Do you want to read more about the subjects or ideas in this book? Want to play cool games or watch videos about the authors who write these books? Then go to **FactHound**. At *www.facthound.com*, you'll be able to do all that, and more. The FactHound website can also send you to other safe Internet sites.

Check it out!